Caillou®

Sleeps Over

Adaptation of the animated series: Nicole Nadeau
Illustrations taken from the animated series

Caillou was very excited. His friend Leo had invited Caillou to sleep over at his house. Caillou couldn't wait to go.

This was the first time Caillou had ever stayed overnight at a friend's house. He ran to his room to get his backpack ready.

Caillou didn't want to forget his dinosaurs, his favorite toy car or his special cardboard sword.

When they were ready to go, Mommy asked Caillou if they had forgotten to pack anything. Clothes, pajamas, toothbrush, teddy bear?
"Teddy!" shouted Caillou. He ran back to his room. How could Caillou sleep at Leo's house without his teddy bear?

On the way to his friend's house, Caillou talked about Leo the whole time. Leo had something absolutely fantastic – a tree house! Caillou and Leo often played there together.

As soon as they arrived, Caillou ran to find Leo, forgetting about Mommy and his stuff in the car. Quickly, the friends climbed the ladder up the tree. When he reached the top, Caillou saw Mommy holding his backpack and overnight bag.

"I have to go now, Caillou," she said. "Have fun, and see you tomorrow."

"Bye, Mommy!" shouted Caillou, waving.

Caillou went back to playing with his friend. He and Leo spent all afternoon in the tree house.

At supper time, Caillou sat down beside Leo and looked around the table.

There were Leo's mommy and daddy, and Leo's big brother. Everybody started eating except Caillou. He didn't feel hungry.

Caillou missed his family.
"Aren't you hungry, Caillou?"
Leo's mommy asked. "Let's see
who finishes first and wins the
race to dessert!"
Caillou felt more like eating
now. Especially dessert.

After supper, Caillou showed Leo his collection of dinosaurs. He felt better while they played. He didn't miss his family so much. Soon it was time to go to bed. Time to stop playing, put on his pajamas and brush his teeth.

But Caillou wanted to go home to his own bed, to his own mommy and daddy. When Leo's mommy turned out the light, Caillou started to cry softly. It was so dark in the bedroom. Leo's mommy came to tuck them in.
"What's the matter, Caillou?" she asked gently, hugging him.

"I want my mommy!" Caillou said.

"I understand, Caillou. You're not used to sleeping away from home. I've got an idea. Why don't we call your mommy on the phone?"

Caillou started feeling better already at the idea of calling home.

"Mommy, I want to come home," he said in a small voice.

"Hi, Caillou. Does Teddy want to come home too?" Mommy asked.

"Teddy!" shouted Caillou.

"Poor Teddy," Mommy said. "He must be feeling very lonely stuck inside your backpack. He was really looking forward to sleeping over at Leo's house."

When Caillou thought about Teddy, he didn't want to go home anymore. He hung up the phone and went to look for Teddy.
He found his backpack and reached inside.
"I found Teddy!" he shouted.
Caillou hugged Teddy very tightly.

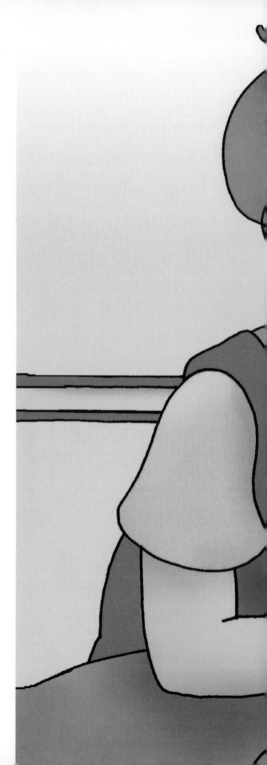

With Teddy warm and cuddly beside him, Caillou was ready to go to sleep. Caillou gave Teddy a big kiss and tucked him in.

Text: adaptation by Nicole Nadeau of the animated series CAILLOU,
produced by DHX Media Inc.
All rights reserved.
Original story written by Matthew Cope
Illustrations taken from the television series CAILLOU and adapted by
Les Studios de La souris Mécanique
Art Direction: Monique Dupras

The PBS KIDS logo is a registered mark of PBS and is used with permission.

Chouette Publishing would like to thank SODEC and the Government of Canada
for their financial support.

Québec ⊞⊞
Books
Tax Credit   Gestion
SODEC

Canadä

Bibliothèque et Archives nationales du Québec and Library and Archives
Canada cataloguing in publication

Nadeau, Nicole, 1956 -
Caillou sleeps over
New ed.
(Clubhouse)
Translation of: Caillou dort chez son ami.
Originally issued in series: Backpack Collection. c1998.
For children aged 3 and up.

ISBN 9782894509074

1. Autonomy (Psychology) - Juvenile literature. 2. Self-actualization
(Psychology) - Juvenile literature. I. Title. II. Series: Clubhouse.

HQ781.5.N3213 2012   j155.25   C2011-942190-9

Printed in China
10 9 8 7 6 5 4 3 2 1 CHO1953 AUG2015